The Music of Erich Zann, The Nameless City, and Nyarlathotep

H. P. Lovecraft

DODO ✺ PRESS

The Music of Erich Zann

by H. P. Lovecraft

The Music of Erich Zann

I have examined maps of the city with the greatest care, yet have never again found the Rue d'Auseil. These maps have not been modern maps alone, for I know that names change. I have, on the contrary, delved deeply into all the antiquities of the place, and have personally explored every region, of whatever name, which could possibly answer to the street I knew as the Rue d'Auseil. But despite all I have done, it remains an humiliating fact that I cannot find the house, the street, or even the locality, where, during the last months of my impoverished life as a student of metaphysics at the university, I heard the music of Erich Zann.

That my memory is broken, I do not wonder; for my health, physical and mental, was gravely disturbed throughout the period of my residence in the Rue d'Auseil, and I recall that I took none of my few acquaintances there. But that I cannot find the place again is both singular and perplexing; for it was within a half-hour's walk of the university and was distinguished by peculiarities which could hardly be forgotten by any one who had been there. I have never met a person who has seen the Rue d'Auseil.

The Rue d'Auseil lay across a dark river bordered by precipitous brick blear-windowed warehouses and spanned by a ponderous bridge of dark stone. It was always shadowy along that river, as if the smoke of neighboring factories shut out the sun perpetually. The river was also odorous with evil stenches which I have never smelled elsewhere, and which may some day help me to find it, since I should recognize them at once. Beyond the bridge were narrow cobbled streets with rails; and then came the ascent, at first gradual, but incredibly steep as the Rue d'Auseil was reached.

I have never seen another street as narrow and steep as the Rue d'Auseil. It was almost a cliff, closed to all vehicles, consisting in several places of flights of steps, and ending at the top in a lofty ivied wall. Its paving was irregular, sometimes stone slabs, sometimes cobblestones, and sometimes bare earth with struggling greenish-grey vegetation. The houses were tall, peaked-roofed, incredibly old, and crazily leaning backward, forward, and sidewise. Occasionally an opposite pair, both leaning forward, almost met across the street like an arch; and certainly they kept most of the light from the ground below. There were a few overhead bridges from house to house across the street.

The inhabitants of that street impressed me peculiarly; At first I thought it was because they were all silent and reticent; but later decided it was because they were all very old. I do not know how I came to live on such a street, but I was not myself when I moved there. I had been living in many poor places, always evicted for want of money; until at last I came upon that tottering house in the Rue d'Auseil kept by the paralytic Blandot. It was the third house from the top of the street, and by far the tallest of them all.

My room was on the fifth story; the only inhabited room there, since the house was almost empty. On the night I arrived I heard strange music from the peaked garret overhead, and the next day asked old Blandot about it. He told me it was an old German viol-player, a strange dumb man who signed his name as Erich Zann, and who played evenings in a cheap theater orchestra; adding that Zann's desire to play in the night after his return from the theater was the reason he had chosen this lofty and isolated garret room, whose single gable window was the only point on the street from which one could look over the terminating wall at the declivity and panorama beyond.

Thereafter I heard Zann every night, and although he kept me awake, I was haunted by the weirdness of his music. Knowing little of the art myself, I was yet certain that none of his harmonies had any relation to music I had heard before; and concluded that he was a composer of highly original genius. The longer I listened, the more I was fascinated, until after a week I resolved to make the old man's acquaintance.

One night as he was returning from his work, I intercepted Zann in the hallway and told him that I would like to know him and be with him when he played. He was a small, lean, bent person, with shabby clothes, blue eyes, grotesque, satyrlike face, and nearly bald head; and at my first words seemed both angered and frightened. My obvious friendliness, however, finally melted him; and he grudgingly motioned to me to follow him up the dark, creaking and rickety attic stairs. His room, one of only two in the steeply pitched garret, was on the west side, toward the high wall that formed the upper end of the street. Its size was very great, and seemed the greater because of its extraordinary barrenness and neglect. Of furniture there was only a narrow iron bedstead, a dingy wash-stand, a small table, a large bookcase, an iron music-rack, and three old-fashioned chairs. Sheets of music were piled in disorder about the floor. The walls were of bare boards, and had probably never known plaster; whilst the abundance of dust and cobwebs made the place seem more deserted than inhabited. Evidently Erich Zann's world of beauty lay in some far cosmos of the imagination.

Motioning me to sit down, the dumb man closed the door, turned the large wooden bolt, and lighted a candle to augment the one he had brought with him. He now removed his viol from its motheaten covering, and taking it, seated himself in the least uncomfortable of the chairs. He did not employ the music-rack, but, offering no choice and playing from memory, enchanted me for over an hour with strains I had never heard before; strains which must have been of his own devising. To describe their exact nature is impossible for one unversed in music. They were a kind of fugue, with recurrent passages of the most captivating quality, but to me were notable for the absence of any of the weird notes I had overheard from my room below on other occasions.

Those haunting notes I had remembered, and had often hummed and whistled inaccurately to myself, so when the player at length laid down his bow I asked him if he would render some of them. As I began my request the wrinkled satyrlike face lost the bored placidity it had possessed during the playing, and seemed to show the same curious mixture of anger and fright which I had noticed when first I accosted the old man. For a moment I was inclined to use persuasion, regarding rather lightly the whims of senility; and even tried to awaken my host's weirder mood by whistling a few of the strains to which I had listened the night before. But I did not pursue this course for more than a moment; for when the dumb musician recognized the whistled air his face grew suddenly distorted with an expression wholly beyond analysis, and his long, cold, bony right hand reached out to stop my mouth and silence the crude imitation. As he did this he further demonstrated his eccentricity by casting a startled glance toward the lone curtained window, as if fearful of some intruder—a glance doubly absurd, since the garret stood high and inaccessible above all the adjacent roofs, this window being the only point on the steep street, as the concierge had told me, from which one could see over the wall at the summit.

The old man's glance brought Blandot's remark to my mind, and with a certain capriciousness I felt a wish to look out over the wide and dizzying panorama of moonlit roofs and city lights beyond the hilltop, which of all the dwellers in the Rue d'Auseil only this crabbed musician could see. I moved toward the window and would have drawn aside the nondescript curtains, when with a frightened rage even greater than before, the dumb lodger was upon me again; this time motioning with his head toward the door as he nervously strove to drag me thither with both hands. Now thoroughly disgusted with my host, I ordered him to release me, and told him I would go at once. His clutch relaxed, and as he saw my disgust and offense, his own anger seemed to subside. He tightened his relaxing grip, but this time in a friendly manner, forcing me into a chair; then with an appearance of wistfulness crossing to the littered table, where he wrote many words with a pencil, in the labored French of a foreigner.

The note which he finally handed me was an appeal for tolerance and forgiveness. Zann said that he was old, lonely, and afflicted with strange fears and nervous disorders connected with his music and with other things. He had enjoyed my listening to his music, and wished I would come again and not mind his eccentricities. But he could not play to another his weird harmonies, and could not bear hearing them from another; nor could he bear having anything in his room touched by an-other. He had not known until our hallway conversation that I could overhear his playing in my room, and now asked me if I would arrange with Blandot to take a lower room where I could not hear him in the night. He would, he wrote, defray the difference in rent.

As I sat deciphering the execrable French, I felt more lenient toward the old man. He was a victim of physical and nervous suffering, as was I; and my metaphysical studies had taught me kindness. In the silence there came a slight sound from the window—the shutter must have rattled in the night wind, and for some reason I started almost as violently as did Erich Zann. So when I had finished reading, I shook my host by the hand, and departed as a friend.

The next day Blandot gave me a more expensive room on the third floor, between the apartments of an aged money-lender and the room of a respectable upholsterer. There was no one on the fourth floor.

It was not long before I found that Zann's eagerness for my company was not as great as it had seemed while he was persuading me to move down from the fifth story. He did not ask me to call on him, and when I did call he appeared uneasy and played listlessly. This was always at night—in the day he slept and would admit no one. My liking for him did not grow, though the attic room and the weird music seemed to hold an odd fascination for me. I had a curious desire to look out of that window, over the wall and down the unseen slope at the glittering roofs and spires which must lie outspread there. Once I went up to the garret during theater hours, when Zann was away, but the door was locked.

What I did succeed in doing was to overhear the nocturnal playing of the dumb old man. At first I would tip-toe up to my old fifth floor, then I grew bold enough to climb the last creaking staircase to the peaked garret. There in the narrow hall, outside the bolted door with the covered keyhole, I often heard sounds which filled me with an indefinable dread—the dread of vague wonder and brooding mystery. It was not that the sounds were hideous, for they were not; but that they held vibrations suggesting nothing on this globe of earth, and that at certain intervals they assumed a symphonic quality which I could hardly conceive as produced by one player. Certainly, Erich Zann was a genius of wild power. As the weeks passed, the playing grew wilder, whilst the old musician acquired an increasing haggardness and furtiveness pitiful to behold. He now refused to admit me at any time, and shunned me whenever we met on the stairs.

Then one night as I listened at the door, I heard the shrieking viol swell into a chaotic babel of sound; a pandemonium which would have led me to doubt my own shaking sanity had there not come from behind that barred portal a piteous proof that the horror was real— the awful, inarticulate cry which only a mute can utter, and which rises only in moments of the most terrible fear or anguish. I knocked repeatedly at the door, but received no response. Afterward I waited in the black hallway, shivering with cold and fear, till I heard the poor musician's feeble effort to rise from the floor by the aid of a chair. Believing him just conscious after a fainting fit, I renewed my rapping, at the same time calling out my name reassuringly. I heard Zann stumble to the window and close both shutter and sash, then stumble to the door, which he falteringly unfastened to admit me. This time his delight at having me present was real; for his distorted face gleamed with relief while he clutched at my coat as a child clutches at its mother's skirts.

Shaking pathetically, the old man forced me into a chair whilst he sank into another, beside which his viol and bow lay carelessly on the floor. He sat for some time inactive, nodding oddly, but having a paradoxical suggestion of intense and frightened listening. Subsequently he seemed to be satisfied, and crossing to a chair by the table wrote a brief note, handed it to me, and returned to the table, where he began to write rapidly and incessantly. The note implored me in the name of mercy, and for the sake of my own curiosity, to wait where I was while he prepared a full account in German of all the marvels and terrors which beset him. I waited, and the dumb man's pencil flew.

It was perhaps an hour later, while I still waited and while the old musician's feverishly written sheets still continued to pile up, that I saw Zann start as from the hint of a horrible shock. Unmistakably he was looking at the curtained window and listening shudderingly. Then I half fancied I heard a sound myself; though it was not a horrible sound, but rather an exquisitely low and infinitely distant musical note, suggesting a player in one of the neighboring houses, or in some abode beyond the lofty wall over which I had never been able to look. Upon Zann the effect was terrible, for, dropping his pencil, suddenly he rose, seized his viol, and commenced to rend the night with the wildest playing I had ever heard from his bow save when listening at the barred door.

It would be useless to describe the playing of Erich Zann on that dreadful night. It was more horrible than anything I had ever overheard, because I could now see the expression of his face, and could realize that this time the motive was stark fear. He was trying to make a noise; to ward something off or drown something out—what, I could not imagine, awesome though I felt it must be. The playing grew fantastic, dehnous, and hysterical, yet kept to the last the qualities of supreme genius which I knew this strange old man possessed. I recognized the air—it was a wild Hungarian dance popular in the theaters, and I reflected for a moment that this was the first time I had ever heard Zann play the work of another composer.

Louder and louder, wilder and wilder, mounted the shrieking and whining of that desperate viol. The player was dripping with an uncanny perspiration and twisted like a monkey, always looking frantically at the curtained window. In his frenzied strains I could almost see shadowy satyrs and bacchanals dancing and whirling insanely through seething abysses of clouds and smoke and lightning. And then I thought I heard a shriller, steadier note that was not from the viol; a calm, deliberate, purposeful, mocking note from far away in the West.

At this juncture the shutter began to rattle in a howling night wind which had sprung up outside as if in answer to the mad playing within. Zann's screaming viol now outdid itself emitting sounds I had never thought a viol could emit. The shutter rattled more loudly, unfastened, and commenced slamming against the window. Then the glass broke shiveringly under the persistent impacts, and the chill wind rushed in, making the candles sputter and rustling the sheets of paper on the table where Zann had begun to write out his horrible secret. I looked at Zann, and saw that he was past conscious observation. His blue eyes were bulging, glassy and sightless, and the frantic playing had become a blind, mechanical, unrecognizable orgy that no pen could even suggest.

A sudden gust, stronger than the others, caught up the manuscript and bore it toward the window. I followed the flying sheets in desperation, but they were gone before I reached the demolished panes. Then I remembered my old wish to gaze from this window, the only window in the Rue d'Auseil from which one might see the slope beyond the wall, and the city outspread beneath. It was very dark, but the city's lights always burned, and I expected to see them there amidst the rain and wind. Yet when I looked from that highest of all gable windows, looked while the candles sputtered and the insane viol howled with the night-wind, I saw no city spread below, and no friendly lights gleamed from remembered streets, but only the blackness of space illimitable; unimagined space alive with motion and music, and having no semblance of anything on earth. And as I stood there looking in terror, the wind blew out both the candles in that ancient peaked garret, leaving me in savage and impenetrable darkness with chaos and pandemonium before me, and the demon madness of that night-baying viol behind me.

I staggered back in the dark, without the means of striking a light, crashing against the table, overturning a chair, and finally groping my way to the place where the blackness screamed with shocking music. To save myself and Erich Zann I could at least try, whatever the powers opposed to me. Once I thought some chill thing brushed me, and I screamed, but my scream could not be heard above that hideous viol. Suddenly out of the blackness the madly sawing bow struck me, and I knew I was close to the player. I felt ahead, touched the back of Zann's chair, and then found and shook his shoulder in an effort to bring him to his senses.

He did not respond, and still the viol shrieked on without slackening. I moved my hand to his head, whose mechanical nodding I was able to stop, and shouted in his ear that we must both flee from the unknown things of the night. But he neither answered me nor abated the frenzy of his unutterable music, while all through the garret strange currents of wind seemed to dance in the darkness and babel. When my hand touched his ear I shuddered, though I knew not why—knew not why till I felt the still face; the ice-cold, stiffened, unbreathing face whose glassy eyes bulged uselessly into the void. And then, by some miracle, finding the door and the large wooden bolt, I plunged wildly away from that glassy-eyed thing in the dark, and from the ghoulish howling of that accursed viol whose fury increased even as I plunged.

Leaping, floating, flying down those endless stairs through the dark house; racing mindlessly out into the narrow, steep, and ancient street of steps and tottering houses; clattering down steps and over cobbles to the lower streets and the putrid canyon-walled river; panting across the great dark bridge to the broader, healthier streets and boulevards we know; all these are terrible impressions that linger with me. And I recall that there was no wind, and that the moon was out, and that all the lights of the city twinkled.

Despite my most careful searches and investigations, I have never since been able to find the Rue d'Auseil. But I am not wholly sorry; either for this or for the loss in undreamable abysses of the closely-written sheets which alone could have explained the music of Erich Zann.

The Nameless City

by H. P. Lovecraft

The Nameless City

When I drew nigh the nameless city I knew it was accursed. I was traveling in a parched and terrible valley under the moon, and afar I saw it protruding uncannily above the sands as parts of a corpse may protrude from an ill-made grave. Fear spoke from the age-worn stones of this hoary survivor of the deluge, this great-grandfather of the eldest pyramid; and a viewless aura repelled me and bade me retreat from antique and sinister secrets that no man should see, and no man else had dared to see..

Remote in the desert of Araby lies the nameless city, crumbling and inarticulate, its low walls nearly hidden by the sands of uncounted ages. It must have been thus before the first stones of Memphis were laid, and while the bricks of Babylon were yet unbaked. There is no legend so old as to give it a name, or to recall that it was ever alive; but it is told of in whispers around campfires and muttered about by grandams in the tents of sheiks so that all the tribes shun it without wholly knowing why. It was of this place that Abdul Alhazred the mad poet dreamed of the night before he sang his unexplained couplet:

> *That is not dead which can eternal lie,*
> *And with strange aeons even death may die.*

I should have known that the Arabs had good reason for shunning the nameless city, the city told of in strange tales but seen by no living man, yet I defied them and went into the untrodden waste with my camel. I alone have seen it, and that is why no other face bears such hideous lines of fear as mine; why no other man shivers so horribly when the night wind rattles the windows. When I came upon it in the ghastly stillness of unending sleep it looked at me, chilly from the rays of a cold moon amidst the desert's heat. And as I returned its look I forgot my triumph at finding it, and stopped still with my camel to wait for the dawn.

For hours I waited, till the east grew grey and the stars faded, and the grey turned to roseate light edged with gold. I heard a moaning and saw a storm of sand stirring among the antique stones though the sky was clear and the vast reaches of desert still. Then suddenly above the desert's far rim came the blazing edge of the sun, seen through the tiny sandstorm which was passing away, and in my fevered state I fancied that from some remote depth there came a crash of musical metal to hail the fiery disc as Memnon hails it from the banks of the Nile. My ears rang and my imagination seethed as I led my camel slowly across the sand to that unvocal place; that place which I alone of living men had seen.

In and out amongst the shapeless foundations of houses and places I wandered, finding never a carving or inscription to tell of these men, if men they were, who built this city and dwelt therein so long ago. The antiquity of the spot was unwholesome, and I longed to encounter some sign or device to prove that the city was indeed fashioned by mankind. There were certain proportions and dimensions in the ruins which I did not like. I had with me many tools, and dug much within the walls of the obliterated edifices; but progress was slow, and nothing significant was revealed. When night and the moon returned I felt a chill wind which brought new fear, so that I did not dare to remain in the city. And as I went outside the antique walls to sleep, a small sighing sandstorm gathered behind me, blowing over the grey stones though the moon was bright and most of the desert still.

I awakened just at dawn from a pageant of horrible dreams, my ears ringing as from some metallic peal. I saw the sun peering redly through the last gusts of a little sandstorm that hovered over the nameless city, and marked the quietness of the rest of the landscape. Once more I ventured within those brooding ruins that swelled beneath the sand like an ogre under a coverlet, and again dug vainly for relics of the forgotten race. At noon I rested, and in the afternoon I spent much time tracing the walls and bygone streets, and the outlines of the nearly vanished buildings. I saw that the city had been mighty indeed, and wondered at the sources of its greatness. To myself I pictured all the spendours of an age so distant that Chaldaea could not recall it, and thought of Sarnath the Doomed, that stood in the land of Mnar when mankind was young, and of Ib, that was carven of grey stone before mankind existed.

All at once I came upon a place where the bed rock rose stark through the sand and formed a low cliff; and here I saw with joy what seemed to promise further traces of the antediluvian people. Hewn rudely on the face of the cliff were the unmistakable facades of several small, squat rock houses or temples; whose interiors might preserve many secrets of ages too remote for calculation, though sandstorms had long effaced any carvings which may have been outside.

Very low and sand-choked were all the dark apertures near me, but I cleared on with my spade and crawled through it, carrying a torch to reveal whatever mysteries it might hold. When I was inside I saw that the cavern was indeed a temple, and beheld plain signs of the race that had lived and worshiped before the desert was a desert. Primitive altars, pillars, and niches, all curiously low, were not absent; and though I saw no sculptures or frescoes, there were many singular stones clearly shaped into symbols by artificial means. The lowness of the chiseled chamber was very strange, for I could hardly kneel upright; but the area was so great that my torch showed only part of it at a time. I shuddered oddly in some of the far corners; for certain altars and stones suggested forgotten rites of terrible, revolting and inexplicable nature and made me wonder what manner of men could have made and frequented such a temple. When I had seen all that the place contained, I crawled out again, avid to find what the temples might yield.

Night had now approached, yet the tangible things I had seen made curiosity stronger than fear, so that I did not flee from the long mooncast shadows that had daunted me when first I saw the nameless city. In the twilight I cleared another aperture and with a new torch crawled into it, finding more vague stones and symbols, though nothing more definite than the other temple had contained. The room was just as low, but much less broad, ending in a very narrow passage crowded with obscure and cryptical shrines. About these shrines I was prying when the noise of a wind and my camel outside broke through the stillness and drew me forth to see what could have frightened the beast.

The moon was gleaming vividly over the primitive ruins, lighting a dense cloud of sand that seemed blown by a strong but decreasing wind from some point along the cliff ahead of me. I knew it was this chilly, sandy wind which had disturbed the camel and was about to lead him to a place of better shelter when I chanced to glance up and saw that there was no wind atop the cliff. This astonished me and made me fearful again, but I immediately recalled the sudden local winds that I had seen and heard before at sunrise and sunset, and judged it was a normal thing. I decided it came from some rock fissure leading to a cave, and watched the troubled sand to trace it to its source; soon perceiving that it came from the black orifice of a temple a long distance south of me, almost out of sight. Against the choking sand-cloud I plodded toward this temple, which as I neared it loomed larger than the rest, and shewed a doorway far less clogged with caked sand. I would have entered had not the terrific force of the icy wind almost quenched my torch. It poured madly out of the dark door, sighing uncannily as it ruffled the sand and spread among the weird ruins. Soon it grew fainter and the sand grew more and more still, till finally all was at rest again; but a presence seemed stalking among the spectral stones of the city, and when I glanced at the moon it seemed to quiver as though mirrored in unquiet waters. I was more afraid than I could explain, but not enough to dull my thirst for wonder; so as soon as the wind was quite gone I crossed into the dark chamber from which it had come.

This temple, as I had fancied from the outside, was larger than either of those I had visited before; and was presumably a natural cavern since it bore winds from some region beyond. Here I could stand quite upright, but saw that the stones and altars were as low as those in the other temples. On the walls and roof I beheld for the first time some traces of the pictorial art of the ancient race, curious curling streaks of paint that had almost faded or crumbled away; and on two of the altars I saw with rising excitement a maze of well-fashioned curvilinear carvings. As I held my torch aloft it seemed to me that the shape of the roof was too regular to be natural, and I wondered what the prehistoric cutters of stone had first worked upon. Their engineering skill must have been vast.

Then a brighter flare of the fantastic flame showed that form which I had been seeking, the opening to those remoter abysses whence the sudden wind had blown; and I grew faint when I saw that it was a small and plainly artificial door chiseled in the solid rock. I thrust my torch within, beholding a black tunnel with the roof arching low over a rough flight of very small, numerous and steeply descending steps. I shall always see those steps in my dreams, for I came to learn what they meant.

At the time I hardly knew whether to call them steps or mere footholds in a precipitous descent. My mind was whirling with mad thoughts, and the words and warning of Arab prophets seemed to float across the desert from the land that men know to the nameless city that men dare not know. Yet I hesitated only for a moment before advancing through the portal and commencing to climb cautiously down the steep passage, feet first, as though on a ladder.

It is only in the terrible phantasms of drugs or delirium that any other man can have such a descent as mine. The narrow passage led infinitely down like some hideous haunted well, and the torch I held above my head could not light the unknown depths toward which I was crawling. I lost track of the hours and forgot to consult my watch, though I was frightened when I thought of the distance I must have been traversing. There were changes of direction and of steepness; and once I came to a long, low, level passage where I had to wriggle my feet first along the rocky floor, holding torch at arm's length beyond my head. The place was not high enough for kneeling. After that were more of the steep steps, and I was still scrambling down interminably when my failing torch died out. I do not think I noticed it at the time, for when I did notice it I was still holding it above me as if it were ablaze. I was quite unbalanced with that instinct for the strange and the unknown which had made me a wanderer upon earth and a haunter of far, ancient, and forbidden places.

In the darkness there flashed before my mind fragments of my cherished treasury of daemonic lore; sentences from Alhazred the mad Arab, paragraphs from the apocryphal nightmares of Damascus, and infamous lines from the delirious *Image du Monde* of Gauthier de Metz. I repeated queer extracts, and muttered of Afrasiab and the daemons that floated with him down the Oxus; later chanting over and over again a phrase from one of Lord Dunsany's tales—"The unreveberate blackness of the abyss." Once when the descent grew amazingly steep I recited something in sing-song from Thomas Moore until I feared to recite more:

> *A reservoir of darkness, black*
> *As witches' cauldrons are, when fill'd*
> *With moon-drugs in th' eclipse distill'd*
> *Leaning to look if foot might pass*
> *Down thro' that chasm, I saw, beneath,*
> *As far as vision could explore,*
> *The jetty sides as smooth as glass,*
> *Looking as if just varnish'd o'er*
> *With that dark pitch the Seat of Death*
> *Throws out upon its slimy shore.*

Time had quite ceased to exist when my feet again felt a level floor, and I found myself in a place slightly higher than the rooms in the two smaller temples now so incalculably far above my head. I could not quite stand, but could kneel upright, and in the dark I shuffled and crept hither and thither at random. I soon knew that I was in a narrow passage whose walls were lined with cases of wood having glass fronts. As in that Palaeozoic and abysmal place I felt of such things as polished wood and glass I shuddered at the possible implications. The cases were apparently ranged along each side of the passage at regular intervals, and were oblong and horizontal, hideously like coffins in shape and size. When I tried to move two or three for further examination, I found that they were firmly fastened.

I saw that the passage was a long one, so floundered ahead rapidly in a creeping run that would have seemed horrible had any eye watched me in the blackness; crossing from side to side occasionally to feel of my surroundings and be sure the walls and rows of cases still stretched on. Man is so used to thinking visually that I almost forgot the darkness and pictured the endless corridor of wood and glass in its low-studded monotony as though I saw it. And then in a moment of indescribable emotion I did see it.

Just when my fancy merged into real sight I cannot tell; but there came a gradual glow ahead, and all at once I knew that I saw the dim outlines of a corridor and the cases, revealed by some unknown subterranean phosphorescence. For a little while all was exactly as I had imagined it, since the glow was very faint; but as I mechanically kept stumbling ahead into the stronger light I realized that my fancy had been but feeble. This hall was no relic of crudity like the temples in the city above, but a monument of the most magnificent and exotic art. Rich, vivid, and daringly fantastic designs and pictures formed a continuous scheme of mural paintings whose lines and colours were beyond description. The cases were of a strange golden wood, with fronts of exquisite glass, and containing the mummified forms of creatures outreaching in grotesqueness the most chaotic dreams of man.

To convey any idea of these monstrosities is impossible. They were of the reptile kind, with body lines suggesting sometimes the crocodile, sometimes the seal, but more often nothing of which either the naturalist or the palaeontologist ever heard. In size they approximated a small man, and their fore-legs bore delicate and evident feet curiously like human hands and fingers. But strangest of all were their heads, which presented a contour violating all known biological principles. To nothing can such things be well compared—in one flash I thought of comparisons as varied as the cat, the bullfrog, the mythic Satyr, and the human being. Not Jove himself had had so colossal and protuberant a forehead, yet the horns and the noselessness and the alligator-like jaw placed things outside all established categories. I debated for a time on the reality of the mummies, half suspecting they were artificial idols; but soon decided they were indeed some palaeogean species which had lived when the nameless city was alive. To crown their grotesqueness, most of them were gorgeously enrobed in the costliest of fabrics, and lavishly laden with ornaments of gold, jewels, and unknown shining metals.

The importance of these crawling creatures must have been vast, for they held first place among the wild designs on the frescoed walls and ceiling. With matchless skill had the artist drawn them in a world of their own, wherein they had cities and gardens fashioned to suit their dimensions; and I could not help but think that their pictured history was allegorical, perhaps shewing the progress of the race that worshiped them. These creatures, I said to myself, were to men of the nameless city what the she-wolf was to Rome, or some totem-beast is to a tribe of Indians.

Holding this view, I could trace roughly a wonderful epic of the nameless city; the tale of a mighty seacoast metropolis that ruled the world before Africa rose out of the waves, and of its struggles as the sea shrank away, and the desert crept into the fertile valley that held it. I saw its wars and triumphs, its troubles and defeats, and afterwards its terrible fight against the desert when thousands of its people—here represented in allegory by the grotesque reptiles—were driven to chisel their way down though the rocks in some marvelous manner to another world whereof their prophets had told them. It was all vividly weird and realistic, and its connection with the awesome descent I had made was unmistakable. I even recognized the passages.

As I crept along the corridor toward the brighter light I saw later stages of the painted epic—the leave-taking of the race that had dwelt in the nameless city and the valley around for ten million years; the race whose souls shrank from quitting scenes their bodies had known so long where they had settled as nomads in the earth's youth, hewing in the virgin rock those primal shrines at which they had never ceased to worship. Now that the light was better I studied the pictures more closely and, remembering that the strange reptiles must represent the unknown men, pondered upon the customs of the nameless city. Many things were peculiar and inexplicable. The civilization, which included a written alphabet, had seemingly risen to a higher order than those immeasurably later civilizations of Egypt and Chaldaea, yet there were curious omissions. I could, for example, find no pictures to represent deaths or funeral customs, save such as were related to wars, violence, and plagues; and I wondered at the reticence shown concerning natural death. It was as though an ideal of immortality had been fostered as a cheering illusion.

Still nearer the end of the passage was painted scenes of the utmost picturesqueness and extravagance: contrasted views of the nameless city in its desertion and growing ruin, and of the strange new realm of paradise to which the race had hewed its way through the stone. In these views the city and the desert valley were shewn always by moonlight, golden nimbus hovering over the fallen walls, and half-revealing the splendid perfection of former times, shown spectrally and elusively by the artist. The paradisal scenes were almost too extravagant to be believed, portraying a hidden world of eternal day filled with glorious cities and ethereal hills and valleys. At the very last I thought I saw signs of an artistic anticlimax. The paintings were less skillful, and much more bizarre than even the wildest of the earlier scenes. They seemed to record a slow decadence of the ancient stock, coupled with a growing ferocity toward the outside world from which it was driven by the desert. The forms of the people—always represented by the sacred reptiles—appeared to be gradually wasting away, though their spirit as shewn hovering above the ruins by moonlight gained in proportion. Emaciated priests, displayed as reptiles in ornate robes, cursed the upper air and all who breathed it; and one terrible final scene shewed a primitive-looking man, perhaps a pioneer of ancient Irem, the City of Pillars, torn to pieces by members of the elder race. I remember how the Arabs fear the nameless city, and was glad that beyond this place the grey walls and ceiling were bare.

As I viewed the pageant of mural history I had approached very closely to the end of the low-ceiled hall, and was aware of a gate through which came all of the illuminating phosphorescence. Creeping up to it, I cried aloud in transcendent amazement at what lay beyond; for instead of other and brighter chambers there was only an illimitable void of uniform radiance, such one might fancy when gazing down from the peak of Mount Everest upon a sea of sunlit mist. Behind me was a passage so cramped that I could not stand upright in it; before me was an infinity of subterranean effulgence.

Reaching down from the passage into the abyss was the head of a steep flight of steps—small numerous steps like those of black passages I had traversed—but after a few feet the glowing vapours concealed everything. Swung back open against the left-hand wall of the passage was a massive door of brass, incredibly thick and decorated with fantastic bas-reliefs, which could if closed shut the whole inner world of light away from the vaults and passages of rock. I looked at the step, and for the nonce dared not try them. I touched the open brass door, and could not move it. Then I sank prone to the stone floor, my mind aflame with prodigious reflections which not even a death-like exhaustion could banish.

As I lay still with closed eyes, free to ponder, many things I had lightly noted in the frescoes came back to me with new and terrible significance—scenes representing the nameless city in its heyday—the vegetations of the valley around it, and the distant lands with which its merchants traded. The allegory of the crawling creatures puzzled me by its universal prominence, and I wondered that it would be so closely followed in a pictured history of such importance. In the frescoes the nameless city had been shewn in proportions fitted to the reptiles. I wondered what its real proportions and magnificence had been, and reflected a moment on certain oddities I had noticed in the ruins. I thought curiously of the lowness of the primal temples and of the underground corridor, which were doubtless hewn thus out of deference to the reptile deities there honoured; though it perforce reduced the worshipers to crawling. Perhaps the very rites here involved crawling in imitation of the creatures. No religious theory, however, could easily explain why the level passages in that awesome descent should be as low as the temples—or lower, since one cold not even kneel in it. As I thought of the crawling creatures, whose hideous mummified forms were so close to me, I felt a new throb of fear. Mental associations are curious, and I shrank from the idea that except for the poor primitive man torn to pieces in the last painting, mine was the only human form amidst the many relics and symbols of the primordial life.

But as always in my strange and roving existence, wonder soon drove out fear; for the luminous abyss and what it might contain presented a problem worthy of the greatest explorer. That a weird world of mystery lay far down that flight of peculiarly small steps I could not doubt, and I hoped to find there those human memorials which the painted corridor had failed to give. The frescoes had pictured unbelievable cities, and valleys in this lower realm, and my fancy dwelt on the rich and colossal ruins that awaited me.

My fears, indeed, concerned the past rather than the future. Not even the physical horror of my position in that cramped corridor of dead reptiles and antediluvian frescoes, miles below the world I knew and faced by another world of eerie light and mist, could match the lethal dread I felt at the abysmal antiquity of the scene and its soul. An ancientness so vast that measurement is feeble seemed to leer down from the primal stones and rock-hewn temples of the nameless city, while the very latest of the astounding maps in the frescoes shewed oceans and continents that man has forgotten, with only here and there some vaguely familiar outlines. Of what could have happened in the geological ages since the paintings ceased and the death-hating race resentfully succumbed to decay, no man might say. Life had once teemed in these caverns and in the luminous realm beyond; now I was alone with vivid relics, and I trembled to think of the countless ages through which these relics had kept a silent deserted vigil.

Suddenly there came another burst of that acute fear which had intermittently seized me ever since I first saw the terrible valley and the nameless city under a cold moon, and despite my exhaustion I found myself starting frantically to a sitting posture and gazing back along the black corridor toward the tunnels that rose to the outer world. My sensations were like those which had made me shun the nameless city at night, and were as inexplicable as they were poignant. In another moment, however, I received a still greater shock in the form of a definite sound—the first which had broken the utter silence of these tomb-like depths. It was a deep, low moaning, as of a distant throng of condemned spirits, and came from the direction in which I was staring. Its volume rapidly grew, till it soon reverberated rightfully through the low passage, and at the same time I became conscious of an increasing draught of old air, likewise flowing from the tunnels and the city above. The touch of this air seemed to restore my balance, for I instantly recalled the sudden gusts which had risen around the mouth of the abyss each sunset and sunrise, one of which had indeed revealed the hidden tunnels to me. I looked at my watch and saw that sunrise was near, so bracing myself to resist the gale that was sweeping down to its cavern home as it had swept forth at evening. My fear again waned low, since a natural phenomenon tends to dispel broodings over the unknown.

More and more madly poured the shrieking, moaning night wind into the gulf of the inner earth. I dropped prone again and clutched vainly at the floor for fear of being swept bodily through the open gate into the phosphorescent abyss. Such fury I had not expected, and as I grew aware of an actual slipping of my form toward the abyss I was beset by a thousand new terrors of apprehension and imagination. The malignancy of the blast awakened incredible fancies; once more I compared myself shudderingly to the only human image in that frightful corridor, the man who was torn to pieces by the nameless race, for in the fiendish clawing of the swirling currents there seemed to abide a vindictive rage all the stronger because it was largely impotent. I think I screamed frantically near the last—I was almost mad—of the howling wind-wraiths. I tried to crawl against the murderous invisible torrent, but I could not even hold my own as I was pushed slowly and inexorably toward the unknown world. Finally reason must have wholly snapped; for I fell babbling over and over that unexplainable couplet of the mad Arab Alhazred, who dreamed of the nameless city:

> *That is not dead which can eternal lie,*
> *And with strange aeons even death may die.*

Only the grim brooding desert gods know what really took place—what indescribable struggles and scrambles in the dark I endured or what Abaddon guided me back to life, where I must always remember and shiver in the night wind till oblivion—or worse—claims me. Monstrous, unnatural, colossal, was the thing—too far beyond all the ideas of man to be believed except in the silent damnable small hours of the morning when one cannot sleep.

I have said that the fury of the rushing blast was infernal—cacodaemoniacal—and that its voices were hideous with the pent-up viciousness of desolate eternities. Presently these voices, while still chaotic before me, seemed to my beating brain to take articulate form behind me; and down there in the grave of unnumbered aeon-dead antiquities, leagues below the dawn-lit world of men, I heard the ghastly cursing and snarling of strange-tongued fiends. Turning, I saw outlined against the luminous aether of the abyss what could not be seen against the dusk of the corridor—a nightmare horde of rushing devils; hate distorted, grotesquely panoplied, half transparent devils of a race no man might mistake— the crawling reptiles of the nameless city.

And as the wind died away I was plunged into the ghoul-pooled darkness of earth's bowels; for behind the last of the creatures the great brazen door clanged shut with a deafening peal of metallic music whose reverberations swelled out to the distant world to hail the rising sun as Memnon hails it from the banks of the Nile.

Nyarlathotep

by H. P. Lovecraft

Nyarlathotep

Nyarlathotep... the crawling chaos... I am the last... I will tell the audient void....

I do not recall distinctly when it began, but it was months ago. The general tension was horrible. To a season of political and social upheaval was added a strange and brooding apprehension of hideous physical danger; a danger widespread and all-embracing, such a danger as may be imagined only in the most terrible phantasms of the night. I recall that the people went about with pale and worried faces, and whispered warnings and prophecies which no one dared consciously repeat or acknowledge to himself that he had heard. A sense of monstrous guilt was upon the land, and out of the abysses between the stars swept chill currents that made men shiver in dark and lonely places. There was a daemoniac alteration in the sequence of the seasons — the autumn heat lingered fearsomely, and everyone felt that the world and perhaps the universe had passed from the control of known gods or forces to that of gods or forces which were unknown.

And it was then that Nyarlathotep came out of Egypt. Who he was, none could tell, but he was of the old native blood and looked like a Pharaoh. The fellahin knelt when they saw him, yet could not say why. He said he had risen up out of the blackness of twenty-seven centuries, and that he had heard messages from places not on this planet. Into the lands of civilisation came Nyarlathotep, swarthy, slender, and sinister, always buying strange instruments of glass and metal and combining them into instruments yet stranger. He spoke much of the sciences – of electricity and psychology — and gave exhibitions of power which sent his spectators away speechless, yet which swelled his fame to exceeding magnitude. Men advised one another to see Nyarlathotep, and shuddered. And where Nyarlathotep went, rest vanished; for the small hours were rent with the screams of nightmare. Never before had the screams of nightmare been such a public problem; now the wise men almost wished they could forbid sleep in the small hours, that the shrieks of cities might less horribly disturb the pale, pitying moon as it glimmered on green waters gliding under bridges, and old steeples crumbling against a sickly sky.

I remember when Nyarlathotep came to my city — the great, the old, the terrible city of unnumbered crimes. My friend had told me of him, and of the impelling fascination and allurement of his revelations, and I burned with eagerness to explore his uttermost mysteries. My friend said they were horrible and impressive beyond my most fevered imaginings; and what was thrown on a screen in the darkened room prophesied things none but Nyarlathotep dared prophesy, and in the sputter of his sparks there was taken from men that which had never been taken before yet which shewed only in the eyes. And I heard it hinted abroad that those who knew Nyarlathotep looked on sights which others saw not.

It was in the hot autumn that I went through the night with the restless crowds to see Nyarlathotep; through the stifling night and up the endless stairs into the choking room. And shadowed on a screen, I saw hooded forms amidst ruins, and yellow evil faces peering from behind fallen monuments. And I saw the world battling against blackness; against the waves of destruction from ultimate space; whirling, churning, struggling around the dimming, cooling sun. Then the sparks played amazingly around the heads of the spectators, and hair stood up on end whilst shadows more grotesque than I can tell came out and squatted on the heads. And when I, who was colder and more scientific than the rest, mumbled a trembling protest about "imposture" and "static electricity," Nyarlathotep drove us all out, down the dizzy stairs into the damp, hot, deserted midnight streets. I screamed aloud that I was not afraid; that I never could be afraid; and others screamed with me for solace. We swore to one another that the city was exactly the same, and still alive; and when the electric lights began to fade we cursed the company over and over again, and laughed at the queer faces we made.

I believe we felt something coming down from the greenish moon, for when we began to depend on its light we drifted into curious involuntary marching formations and seemed to know our destinations though we dared not think of them. Once we looked at the pavement and found the blocks loose and displaced by grass, with scarce a line of rusted metal to shew where the tramways had run. And again we saw a tram-car, lone, windowless, dilapidated, and almost on its side. When we gazed around the horizon, we could not find the third tower by the river, and noticed that the silhouette of the second tower was ragged at the top. Then we split up into narrow columns, each of which seemed drawn in a different direction. One disappeared in a narrow alley to the left, leaving only the echo of a shocking moan. Another filed down a weed-choked subway entrance, howling with a laughter that was mad. My own column was sucked toward the open country, and presently I felt a chill which was not of the hot autumn; for as we stalked out on the dark moor, we beheld around us the hellish moon-glitter of evil snows. Trackless, inexplicable snows, swept asunder in one direction only, where lay a gulf all the blacker for its glittering walls. The column seemed very thin indeed as it plodded dreamily into the gulf. I lingered behind, for the black rift in the green-litten snow was frightful, and I thought I had heard the reverberations of a disquieting wail as my companions vanished; but my power to linger was slight. As if beckoned by those who had gone before, I half-floated between the titanic snowdrifts, quivering and afraid, into the sightless vortex of the unimaginable.

Screamingly sentient, dumbly delirious, only the gods that were can tell. A sickened, sensitive shadow writhing in hands that are not hands, and whirled blindly past ghastly midnights of rotting creation, corpses of dead worlds with sores that were cities, charnel winds that brush the pallid stars and make them flicker low. Beyond the worlds vague ghosts of monstrous things; half-seen columns of unsanctified temples that rest on nameless rocks beneath space and reach up to dizzy vacua above the spheres of light and darkness. And through this revolting graveyard of the universe the muffled, maddening beating of drums, and thin, monotonous whine of blasphemous flutes from inconceivable, unlighted chambers beyond Time; the detestable pounding and piping whereunto dance slowly, awkwardly, and absurdly the gigantic, tenebrous ultimate gods — the blind, voiceless, mindless gargoyles whose soul is Nyarlathotep.

Lightning Source UK Ltd.
Milton Keynes UK
14 August 2010

158420UK00001B/69/P

9 781409 936817